Welcome to

CREEPERS® Mysteries

I hope you brought a flashlight...

CREEPERS® Mysteries

The series that has everyone *talking*...

from **Movies for the Ear®**

Haunted Cattle Drive

Creepers Mysteries—Book 1

Book & Movie for the Ear Script

Haunted Cattle Drive, The Audio

Audie Award Winner for Best Original Program

from the Audio Publishers Association

Toadies

Creepers Mysteries—Book 2

Book & Movie for the Ear Script

Screams at Maybe Mansion

Creepers Mystery Party Game

This copy of

CREEPERS® Mysteries

Book 2

Toadies

belongs to:

____

Your Autograph

Published by Movies for the Ear, LLC

Printed in the United States of America. For information, address Movies for the Ear, LLC, 8362 Tamarack Village, Ste. 119-327, Saint Paul, MN 55125
Cover art ©2010 Movies for the Ear, LLC®

Movies for the Ear® is a registered trademark of Movies for the Ear, LLC.

Library of Congress Cataloging-in-Publication Data
Anderson, Connie Kingrey.
Toadies - Creepers Mysteries series - Book 2 / by Connie Kingrey Anderson
Summary: Harry, Gillian and Arvin, along with their drama club, throw a Halloween party at the Old Hamstead Farm. They are drawn into the farm's legend, and the curse of a jealous witch and her toadies.

ISBN 978-1-935793-03-8 (paperback)
ISBN 978-1-935793-04-5 (E-book)

[1.Halloween – Fiction. 2. Legends – Fiction. 3. Toads – Fiction.
4. Performing Arts.]
I. Anderson, Connie Kingrey. II Title. III. Series

Library of Congress Control Number: 2012930439

Visit us at www.creepersmysteries.com

Dedication

To Vampirus, one of the stars of the Creepers Mystery Party Game: *Screams at Maybe Mansion*...

***The* Star.**

...Huh? What are *you* doing here? No, Vampirus. On a dedication, only *I* write.

Except, of course, when you need correcting...

Correcting?! There are eight suspects in *Screams at Maybe Mansion.* So there are *eight* stars.

Yes, but *I* stand out above the rest.

You're 6½ feet tall...

Funny.

What was I thanking you for again?

For the incredible star quality I bring to Creepers Mystery Party Game: *Screams at Maybe Mansion.*

CUT!!

CREEPERS® Mysteries

Toadies

THE BOOK

Toadies—The Book

Turn the lights down low, and crank the fun up high!
Read it with a flashlight, if you dare!

CREEPERS® Mysteries

Toadies

MOVIE FOR THE EAR SCRIPT

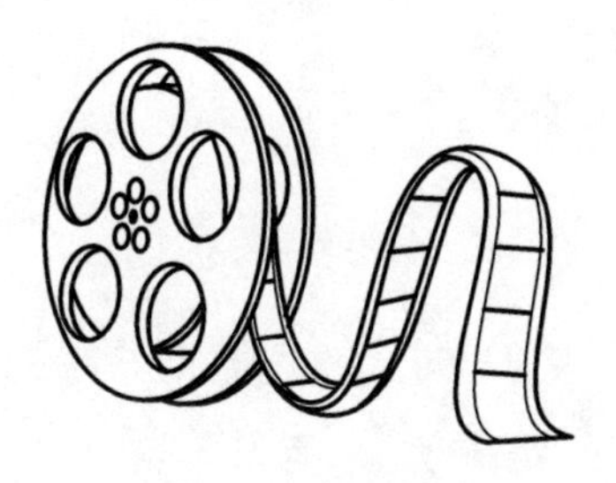

Welcome to

CREEPERS® Mysteries

Toadies

The Book

By Connie Kingrey Anderson

Cover art by B.J. Nartker

Movies for the Ear® Publishers

Chapter 1

What's a Toadie?

There's a low rumbling in the woods behind Hamstead Farm. What's out there?

Nothing that can be seen. The pitch black night covers up the bare trees and prickly bushes that lie just beyond the field. There's not a sliver of moonlight to see by.

But wait, in the darkness there's something small, beady and blinking. Are those eyes watching from the woods? They could be...or maybe they're just blinking shadows.

The rumbling grows louder, and it turns into an eerie sound that's not easy to recognize. It sounds like toads croaking—but not ordinary toads. Their croaks are distorted, as if they're bouncing off the sides of a huge metal funnel.

The toads' beady eyes glow, then disappear into the black night.

Hop, thud, brush...

They move toward the ancient oak tree, the one with the glowing knothole in the trunk. They grunt as they leap and land with heavy thuds. Then strangely, there's the wispy sound of broom bristles brushing away their tracks.

Hop, thud, brush...

"Arvin, do you know what a toadie is?" Harry asked. The two boys slammed their metal lockers shut and made their way down the crowded school hallway.

"Well of course," Arvin said in his know-it-all voice. "Doesn't everybody?"

Arvin had no idea, and Harry knew it.

"Say there's a big bully," Harry began. "All the guys that hang around him, the junior bullies, they aren't bullies at all. They just do what the big bully says. So they're toadies."

"Toadies, huh?" Arvin pondered this for a moment. "What if a guy is just a junior bully, but he thinks he's a big bully?"

"He's still a toadie," Harry answered as he moved through the clumps of kids.

"Ouch!" a girl screeched at the end of the hallway.

"You stepped on my foot Mondo!" She glared after a big kid whose scruffy bangs covered half of his sunglasses. Mondo ignored the girl, and kept shoving and elbowing kids out of his path. "What a jerk," she muttered to her friend. Her friend nodded.

"How about Mondo?" Arvin asked, after he sidestepped the leather-clad tornado.

"Mondo?" Harry shook his head and cracked a smile. "He thinks he's tough like his big brother, but he's just his brother's toadie."

They both watched as Mondo made his way down the hall. He was a big, lumbering, tough guy. He liked to hang out with his brother's older crowd. But at school with kids his own age, he was usually alone. Today he wore his brother's leather jacket. It should have ended at his waist, but instead, hung down past his knees. The long sleeves flapped when he moved, making him look like a deranged penguin.

Suddenly Mondo stopped and plucked a large drawing from the hands of Harry's sister, Gillian. "Ooooh! Look at this!" Mondo threw the drawing in the air and punched it as it floated back down.

"Hey, give it back!" Gillian cried. "Mondo! Give it back!" She jumped up and grabbed for it. But Mondo bounced it just out of her reach.

"Wow! This drawing is so cool, Gillian, I could almost puke!" He shoved his fist into the crinkled paper one more time.

"Mondo! Stop it!! You're going to wreck it! Mondo! Give it here!"

Mondo only laughed. "I better put this garbage *in* the garbage. You don't want to be a litter bug, Gillian."

"Mondo! Don't you dare put my drawing in the garbage! MONDOOOOOO!!!" Gillian screamed.

"Harry," Arvin said calmly, "we better help your sister."

Harry nodded, and they both knew that "we" meant "Harry." Harry picked up his pace and headed down the hall toward the ruckus. Just then, the bell rang, and groups of kids broke apart and headed toward their classrooms.

"Oh, saved by the bell!" Mondo shouted in a mocking tone. "Here's your stupid drawing, Gillian. What do I want with it anyway?" He tossed the wrinkled paper at her.

She grabbed it and glared at him. Then she smoothed the drawing gently, as if petting a cat.

When her gaze drifted up, Gillian was surprised to see Mondo still standing there. He had a weird expression on his face. What was it? He couldn't be *jealous* of her drawing, could he? Or maybe...

Then, as quickly as it appeared, his sad dog expression faded. He turned and lumbered down the hall, looking for more conquests. With each step, he bounced up and down on the balls of his feet, making his curly black head pop up and down through the crowd.

"Look at him hop!" Arvin laughed, now that he was out of Mondo's punching range.

Gillian turned to Arvin. "Thanks for being such a *big* help," she said sarcastically.

"Oh, it was nothing." Arvin smirked. "So Gillian," "What are you trying to *say* with this drawing?" He examined the paper like an art critic.

Gillian rolled her eyes. She had red hair just like her brother Harry, and was short like Arvin, which she hoped would change soon. Before long, one of them would have to have a growth spurt. She better be first.

"If you must know Arvin," she said, "it's a drawing of how to decorate the old Hamstead Farm for the Drama Club's Halloween Party.

"Not bad. What's that thing?" Arvin pointed to a curly line.

"It's a prickly old vine that we're going to wind up the staircase. I drew everything just where I think it should go." Gillian couldn't help beaming, even if it was to Arvin. Her plan was perfect, and she was bursting at the seams to get started. "We can put pumpkins right along the doorway, haystacks over here, and cobwebs and paper skeletons will hang from the ceiling." She smiled broadly.

"Spooooky!" Harry said with a smile. He knew she had put a ton of work into her plan.

"I just hope Mr. Chad picks me to be the decorating

chairperson." Gillian folded the drawing carefully and placed it in her notebook.

"With that drawing? You've got it in the bag." Harry gave her an encouraging nod, then motioned for them to move along. "Come on, let's get to the Drama Club meeting."

"I just hope Mondo's not there," Gillian said.

"Mondo? He's a toadie," Arvin and Harry said at the same time.

Gillian looked puzzled. "What's a toadie?"

Outside, the schoolyard was empty. But in the grass, beady eyes were blinking.

Hop, thud, brush...

Chapter 2
The Legend of Hamstead Farm

Mr. Chad, the drama teacher, taped a hazy, black and white photo of an old stone farmhouse on his classroom wall. He was a thin man with a pinched face and stringy shoulder-length hair. He turned toward the students, pushed his round wire-rimmed glasses up on his pointed nose, then cleared his throat. “Welcome everyone, come on in and have a seat. We’re just getting started.”

The noise in the room peaked with chairs scraping across the wooden floor and kids shouting across the room. Then everyone quickly found a place to sit, and the room quieted down.

“Now, before we assign committees for the Halloween party, we’re going to read through the play that the Drama Club will be performing,” Mr. Chad said. “It’s just a little something I wrote. Although, I know I’m not as talented a writer as your previous drama teacher,

Mr. Goldman. I'm sure you all know that Mr. Goldman has his play on Broadway and lots of money in his pocket..."

"Not too jealous, is he?" Arvin whispered to Harry.

"Really!" Harry nodded.

"Shhh...," Gillian said.

"I'm sorry, I got carried away." Mr. Chad cleared his throat again. "Now, you all know the local legend of Hamstead Farm, which is where we'll be having our Halloween party." He tapped the photo on the wall with his long index finger. "So, regardless of whether or not you believe the legend, it makes a great play for Halloween.

"As the actors read through the play, the rest of you close your eyes. Pretend that you are at Hamstead Farm that very Halloween night in 1824. Imagine that you hear all the sounds–the hissing wind, the howling of wolves...and the voices of witches. Let's begin."

And with that, several students, who had already been assigned their parts, stood up in front of the class. They opened their play books, *The Legend of Hamstead Farm,* and began to read their lines.

The Legend of Hamstead Farm

NARRATOR: It's All Hallow's Eve in 1824. The sky is ominous. Dark clouds pass over the moon. Crows call, flapping wings swoop down, then fade into the distance.

A stone farmhouse and barn can be seen in the flicker of moonlight. The fields are full of withered and dead cornstalks. Far off in the distance, over gently rolling hills, is a gloomy woods.

What's that? Are those eyes watching from the woods? Or maybe they're just blinking shadows.

A sudden wind hisses around the farmhouse, beating branches against the windows and rattling doors on their hinges. It's not a safe night for man or beast...or witch.

A single lantern glows in the side window of the stone farmhouse. Through the drawn curtain, we see shadows of a man and a woman sitting at a table. In the barn, the animals know there is danger in the air.

HUSBAND: My Goodwife, the cows do not give milk, the hens have stopped laying eggs, and the corn has all withered in the field.

GOODWIFE: Rest assured, dear husband. Things will soon be better.

HUSBAND: You are truly a good and hopeful wife. But our efforts are in vain. Listen to the animals wail.

GOODWIFE: We have been cursed by my sister, the Evil Witch. Go to bed now and rest, husband. When the cock crows in the morning, all will be well again.

NARRATOR: By the moon's glow, a large toadie hops along the dirt path toward the barn. A floating broom follows the toadie, sweeping away its tracks. Hop, thud, brush...hop, thud, brush.

The farm animals moan. Suddenly, the Goodwife appears. She carries a lantern and a shaker of salt. She speaks to the toadie.

GOODWIFE: Good evening, Evil Witch. I see you are disguised as one of your toadies.

NARRATOR: The toadie stops and the floating broom falls to the ground. The Goodwife quickly throws salt on the toadie, then flashes the lantern on it. The light sizzles on the toadie's skin, making it immobile. The Goodwife quickly scoops it up.

GOODWIFE: Ride in my apron, toadie, across the field to the gnarled oak tree.

NARRATOR: In an instant, she is at the tree. She drops her apron and lets the toadie fall to the ground.

GOODWIFE: Now, watch as I pour a circle of salt around the tree. Inside you go.

NARRATOR: A mist with a sickening green glow clouds the tree. Then it fades, revealing a woman all dressed in black. She is the Evil Witch.

EVIL WITCH: Hello sister. You are quite convincing in your role as the Goodwife of Hamstead Farm. Doesn't your husband know you are a witch just like me?

GOODWIFE: A witch, yes, but not like you. Our father always knew you would use your powers for evil, and I would use my powers for good.

EVIL WITCH: And because of that, father left you Hamstead Farm! It should have been mine! See this small wooden farmhouse I hold in my hand? It's Hamstead Farm.

NARRATOR: The Evil Witch throws the miniature farmhouse to the ground and it bursts into flames.

EVIL WITCH: It *was* Hamstead Farm! (wicked laughter)

GOODWIFE: Stop! It is now my turn to stop the burn. Fire, be gone!

NARRATOR: In an instant, the Goodwife's spell puts the fire out.

EVIL WITCH: You aren't going to let me have any fun, are you?

GOODWIFE: Why let your jealousy destroy the very farm you wanted?

EVIL WITCH: Because my jealousy rules! If I can't have Hamstead Farm, then neither will you!

GOODWIFE: Your evil jealousy has no power here.

NARRATOR: The Evil Witch is furious. Her body sizzles and smoke rises from beneath her black robe.

EVIL WITCH: Jealousy fuels my evil! It empowers me! It will destroy Hamstead Farm and those in it!

NARRATOR: The Evil Witch lunges toward the Goodwife. But when she crosses the salt circle, she is flung back against the tree with a forceful gust, as if hit by an electrical current.

EVIL WITCH: Aaahh!!

GOODWIFE: This spell shall imprison your jealous

spirit in the tree. This poisonous vine shall be the lock and key.

NARRATOR: The Evil Witch melts into the tree with a sucking noise.

EVIL WITCH: Aaahh!!

GOODWIFE: Goodbye, jealous sister. Good riddance, Evil Witch.

NARRATOR: The Goodwife turns and walks through the field toward the farmhouse. In a knothole in the craggy bark, there is one yellow evil eye watching the Goodwife as she disappears into the distance.

The end.

Mr. Chad, still with his eyes closed, smiled proudly and softly repeated, "The End."

Then he opened his eyes and stood up. "Thank you everyone for those fine performances. You can take your seats."

Once they were all settled, Mr. Chad pulled a piece of paper from his folder. "Okay Drama Club, here are the committees for the Halloween Party." He looked down at the paper and read, "Decorating Committee...."

Gillian sat up expectantly.
"...Harry is the Chairperson."
"HARRY??!!"

Chapter 3
The Javelin

"Hey Hairball! I heard you choked at the track meet! Did it sound like this, Hairball?" Mondo coughed as if he was bringing up a big gooey wad, then doubled over in laughter.

Harry felt his neck and face turning red.

"Harry, don't listen to Mondo, he's a dweeb," Arvin said. He turned toward Mondo who was propped on his bike at the edge of the track field, looking every bit the pudgy sideliner. "Hey Mondo!" he hollered. "I didn't even see you in the track meet, so shut up!"

"Harry, the Hairball. Choke, choke!" Mondo wrenched obnoxiously, then laughed even louder.

Harry scowled as he watched Mondo's antics. Why did he have to be such a jerk? Harry wished he could let the hot air out of Mondo's big inflated head, and watch it sputter and spin like a deflated balloon...Arvin interrupted his thoughts. "Harry, how come you're out here practicing on a Saturday?" he asked. "Do you see anybody else out here throwing a stick?"

"Javelin," Harry corrected him. Although he didn't have an actual javelin, and instead, was using a long stick that looked like a broom handle.

"Javelin," Arvin repeated. "Not only is it Saturday, it's Halloween. The party's tonight. We've got stuff to do."

"After I choked at last week's track meet, I've got to practice. Just one more throw and then we'll go."

Arvin nodded. "Alright, close your eyes."

"What?"

"I'm coaching you," Arvin said. "This is what coaches do. Close your eyes."

"I don't see how that's going to work, Arvin. Looking where I'm throwing could be the key to this whole thing," Harry said sarcastically.

"You're visualizing," Arvin protested. "All the big athletes do it. Statistics show that if you close your eyes..."

"Alright, alright already, they're closed."

"Now, see yourself throwing the stick," Arvin said.

"Javelin," Harry corrected.

"Javelin. Watch it soaring through the air. Do you see it?"

Harry opened his eyes and looked at Arvin. "No," he said dryly.

"You've got to really concentrate, Harry. Close your eyes and try again. See it? There it goes, soaring high into the air. It's making the most perfect arch against the blue sky. See it...see it, flying long and far, and then it drops perfectly onto the target, effortlessly. Just like it was meant to do. It's a perfect throw Harry! Just perfect!"

A big smile spread across Harry's face, his eyes still closed. "Yeah, yeah...it was perfect!"

"O.K., don't lose that image," Arvin said. "Slowly open your eyes and throw that stick."

"Javelin."

"Javelin," Arvin repeated. "Are you ready?"

Harry opened his eyes slowly, still in the moment. "Yeah, I'm ready." He took a deep breath.

"Throw it!" Arvin ordered.

Harry stepped forward, heaved the stick with all his might, and let go.

"HAAAAAIRBALL!"

"Ugh! Oh no...." Harry faltered, he turned toward the sound—and the stick went with him! It was soaring straight toward Mondo!

"Aaahh!!!" Mondo screamed.

Harry and Arvin froze. Mondo's wide eyes crossed as the stick whizzed toward his nose. At the last possible moment, Mondo ducked, and the stick went soaring over his head.

Harry and Arvin looked at each other, then at Mondo, who was crouched with his hands over his greasy locks. Was he alright?

Mondo slowly rose, blinked, and shook his head like a dog trying to get water out of its ears. Fortunately for Harry, it was only Mondo's pride that needed Band-Aids.

When he finally recovered, Mondo scrunched his angry red face and balled up his fists. Then he reached for his bike and pounded it upright on the pavement. He let out a bloodcurdling bellow as he jumped on his pedal and missed, leaving it to spin in circles as he stumbled forward. He roared even louder.

"Come on! Let's get out of here!" Harry pulled Arvin toward their bikes, which were on the other side of the fence. "Hurry up! Hurry up! He's coming around the fence. He's really snorting."

"I'm trying, I'm trying," Arvin panted, as Mondo's spinning wheels headed straight toward them. "We're going to be history!"

"Mondooo!" a nasal voice called from the parking lot. They all turned to see Mr. Chad standing by his car with the trunk open. Mondo's bike brakes squealed and his tires skidded to a stop.

"Mondo, could you help me load the party supplies?" Mr. Chad asked, as if he had bumped into Mondo on a Sunday stroll in the park. He waved his hand toward the boxes and bags stacked on the pavement by the school's rear entrance.

Mondo gulped. "Uh, sure, Mr. Chad."

"Wow!" A big grin spread over Arvin's face. "Saved by the drama teacher!"

Little did Arvin and Harry know that it would soon be the drama teacher who would need to be saved...

Hop, thud, brush...

Chapter 4
Halloween Decorations

Harry and Arvin parked their bikes in front of the old Hamstead Farmhouse. It wasn't hard to believe that this creepy stone house had been built two-hundred years ago. The windows looked like skeleton eyes. Bare tree branches hung like long fingernails over the roof, scratching it when the wind blew.

"How come we're the first ones here?" Arvin asked.

"Unlucky I guess." Harry picked up his backpack, but he didn't move.

"You know, we could leave and come back after the other kids get here," Arvin offered, getting back on his bike. "I don't mind saying that being here alone gives me the creeps."

Black crows cawed and flapped overhead. The sun was setting fast, casting eerie shadows all around them.

Harry took a deep breath. "Nah, let's just get it over

with. By the time we gather the decorations, everyone else will be here."

The sky was a misty gray now. But the full moon gave Harry and Arvin just enough light to make their way through the field to the woods. There they found what they were looking for—colorful fall leaves. Plus, there was a gnarled old oak tree with a large, prickly vine around it—just what Gillian ordered.

The low sound of toads croaking filled the air.

Harry and Arvin opened their backpacks, took out heavy gloves and big lawn bags, and set to work. But the night made them uneasy. Each time they picked up a handful of leaves, they searched the woods with their eyes. There was something out there in the black patches that gave them the shivers, but they didn't know what it was exactly.

It wasn't too long before they saw flickering car headlights and wandering flashlights at the farmhouse. "Oh, good! They're here!" Arvin hollered.

Then he saw trouble walking through the field toward them. "Uh, oh. Here comes Gillian, and she doesn't look too happy."

Harry could feel his sister's wrath halfway across the field. "Hey Gillian!" he shouted. "We found some great decorations for you." He put on a big grin and pointed toward the vine. "Check this out!"

Gillian wasn't having any of it. She stomped up to

them with her brows furrowed and her bottom lip jutting out.

"What's the matter Gillian?" Arvin asked innocently, as if he didn't know.

Ignoring him, she whirled around to face Harry. "Why did Mr. Chad pick *you* for the decorating chairperson? It should have been me! *I* did all this work."

"Gillian, relax. He only picked me because I'm tall. I can put decorations up high."

"Sure," she said through gritted teeth, and she stepped back toward the gnarled old tree. Why do you always get everything, Harry? Everything is always Harry, Harry, HARRY!"

Behind Gillian's head, there was a faint glow of a yellow eye peering out of the tree's knothole. A toad hopped on Gillian's shoe. She kicked her foot and sent it flying. Then, without another word, she turned and trudged back to the farmhouse.

"Boy, she was really mad," Harry said.

"Jealous," Arvin muttered under his breath.

"We'll decorate everything just like her drawing. That should make her happy." Harry put on a thick glove and tried to yank the prickly vine off the tree. But it wouldn't budge. "Ugh! This thing is really thick."

"Hey..." Arvin stopped and looked around. "Did it just get dark really fast?"

"Yeah. Yeah it did." Harry looked up at the hazy gray

clouds that had drifted over the moon. "We better hurry up."

A toad hopped on Arvin's shoe. He shook his foot to get it off, then slowly looked around. "I have a feeling we're not alone," he whispered.

Suddenly, out of the darkness, a half dozen toads appeared. They stared at him with beady eyes. They didn't move. They barely blinked. Arvin froze. "What's with these t..t..toads all of a sudden?" he whispered.

Harry slowly turned in a circle, the toads surrounded them both now. Their beady eyes almost floated in the dark. "This is really weird." Harry backed away. "Let's get our decorations and get out of here."

Arvin shoved leaves into his bag at a feverish pace.

Harry made one last attempt to break the vine, but it was no use. "We need a knife."

The wind began to howl. The toads croaked louder and louder...then started to move toward Harry and Arvin...closer and closer...

Hop, thud, brush...

"What are they doing?" Arvin squeaked.

"Ah...Ah...I don't know," Harry gasped. "I've never seen anything like it."

The eerie, distorted croaks increased in volume as more and more toads appeared out of the dark woods.

Hop, thud, brush...

They moved closer, and closer...

Suddenly, a high-pitched nasal sound rose out of the field.

"Harry? Arvin? Are you out there?"

"Whew! It's Mr. Chad!" Arvin cried in relief. He squinted to see their teacher approaching through the dark field. Mr. Chad was already in his costume. He was the famous playwright Shakespeare, and wore a cape and goatee.

"Yeah, we're here! We're over here!" Arvin's voice cracked.

Mr. Chad's footsteps crunched on the field's dry cornstalks. As he came nearer, the toads retreated into the woods. Whew! Harry and Arvin were saved.

"Oh!" Mr. Chad said, startled. "There you are. Excuse me for stepping on your foot, Arvin."

"That wasn't my foot." Arvin looked at the patches of moving grass and leaves. He knew exactly what Mr. Chad had stepped on.

"We want to wrap this vine around the staircase for the party," Harry explained, a little too fast. "But it's thick and we need a knife." His eyes darted toward the toads hidden in the leaves. They had stopped moving.

"That's a gnarly old tree isn't it? Hmmm..." Mr. Chad stepped back and took it all in. "Why don't you boys go back and get started with the other decorations. I've got a pocket knife, I'll get the vine."

Arvin snatched up his bag of leaves and sprinted toward the farmhouse before Mr. Chad had even finished talking. Harry was right behind him.

But in the middle of the field, Harry suddenly stopped and looked back. Mr. Chad was all alone in the creepy woods. He could take care of himself...couldn't he? Of course he could, he was a teacher. Harry continued walking. Then he looked back again. He couldn't see Mr. Chad now, the moon had passed under the clouds. Just what was going on with those toads anyway?

"Come on Harry!" Arvin yelled. And after one last glance, Harry turned and ran with Arvin.

Back at the gnarly old tree, Mr. Chad took out his pocket knife and began to saw away. "Ugh, this vine really is tough," he muttered to himself. Then he stopped, let the knife drop feebly to his side, and shook his head. "What am I doing out here in the middle of nowhere, in the dark, sticking myself with this prickly vine? While tonight, Mr. Goldman is sitting in a Broadway theatre watching his own play... Ouch! This vine is sharp... Why couldn't my play be on Broadway? It's not fair. Why does Mr. Goldman get all the breaks, and not me?"

The yellow evil eye in the knothole glowed. It whirled in its socket, straining to see beyond the tight hole. It watched every movement Mr. Chad made. The evil eye grew brighter, then faded. It glowed more brightly still, before fading again. This continued, back and forth, glowing then diming, in a steady, pulsing rhythm.

Mr. Chad sawed, and pulled, and struggled to free the vine from the tree. He was huffing and puffing, and stopped to catch his breath. Beads of sweat covered his forehead and upper lip. "This is no ordinary vine," he gasped. "One more try, and then I'm giving up."

He took one last, deep breath, and with everything he could muster, plunged the pocket knife into the vine. This time, the ferocious jab punctured it, and a high-pitched, hypnotic sound seeped out.

Next, a green mist was released from the vine's wound. It smoked and curled around Mr. Chad's head, then swirled around his body until it covered him. He coughed and spit, and gasped for air. Then all was silent, because Mr. Chad was no longer there...

Slowly, the prickly vine released its hold and peeled away from the gnarly old tree.

The yellow evil eye in the knothole blinked. Then a second eye appeared, and it blinked too.

The bark began to bubble and roll in small waves, forming the face of a woman—no, of a witch—pushing her way out. "Aaahh!!"

Chapter 5
The Evil Witch of Hamstead Farm

With bloodcurdling screams and hideous howls, the Evil Witch rammed her knee and shoulder through the hard tree trunk. The wood cracked like snapped bones, showering the sky with splinters.

When the last of the putrid green mist faded, there she stood. Her dark robe was the same, but the skin under it was still covered in bark. Her fingers were wispy branches. Her grotesque face was gnarled, rough and pocked with knotholes. The only human thing about her was her evil yellow eyes.

She started toward the farmhouse, placing one stump-like leg in front of the other. Suddenly, she was pushed back against the gnarled old tree, as if hit by electric current.

"Aaahh!" she wailed.

A thin line of fire sizzled around the tree, recreating

the age-old circle of salt placed there by the Goodwife of Hamstead Farm.

"Removing the vine removed only part of the curse!" The Evil Witch spit the words out like venom. Then she stopped, turned, and raised her left eyebrow. "Aaahh... the woods are sprinkled with bright beady eyes and familiar shadows." Her evil smile exposed her long, hideous teeth. "I have summoned you, my loyal toadies, to break the curse which has held me prisoner in this tree for hundreds of years."

The toadies moved closer. Hop, thud, brush...

"First, I will drop three branches from this tree. When they hit the ground, small brooms they will be." The Evil Witch waved the twigs that were her fingers. Branches suddenly dropped from the tree, and with a magical burst, they became brooms.

"Now, toadies, take these brooms. Use them as wands to ZAP three jealous souls. Put them in the tree to set me free. Put them in the tree instead of me."

The dead, crunchy leaves rippled around the Evil Witch. "Toadies, remember–deliver them by midnight, and beware of the light."

As clouds passed in front of the moon, the toadies hopped through the dry woods. In the distance, the lights of Hamstead Farm glowed.

Chapter 6
Party Crashers

The crumbling old farmhouse had been transformed into the perfect place for a Halloween party. Pumpkins and haystacks filled the main room. Cobwebs and skeletons hung from the ceiling. The only thing missing from Gillian's decorating plan was the prickly vine winding up the staircase…

Arvin and Harry, decked out in their pirate costumes, surveyed the room. "The decorations turned out pretty well, don't you think?" Arvin asked, as he adjusted the bandana on his head.

"Yeah. I sure hope Gillian likes it." Harry looked around. "Hey, where is she?"

"She must be putting on her costume. What's she wearing?" Arvin asked.

"A long dress, an apron, and an old-fashioned bonnet. She's the Goodwife of Hamstead Farm. There are two other girls with the same costume. They really got into the legend of this old place."

Outside, the toadies' rumblings surrounded the farmhouse, but were drowned out by the loud party music.

Hop, thud, brush...

Just then, Gillian swept into the room in her long dress, looking frantic. She pushed her way through the crowd toward Harry and Arvin. "Harry!" she shouted. "Where's Mr. Chad? It's time to start the play!!"

"The last time I saw him he was in the woods cutting the vine." Harry felt even more guilty now about leaving his teacher out there alone.

"Hey, he never brought that vine." Arvin raised his eyebrows and looked at Harry. "Maybe he never came back..."

Outside, the rumblings grew louder and closer.

Hop, thud, brush...

"What if something happened to him?" Gillian was worried, but also impatient. "We can't start the play without him."

"Let's look around. What's his costume?" Harry asked.

"A black cape and a little goatee. He was dressed as Shakespeare, the famous playwright," Gillian said.

"Come to think of it, he was wearing that costume when he came out to the woods." Arvin looked at Harry again.

"Maybe we should go out to that tree and look around," Harry suggested.

Suddenly, the lights went out in the old farmhouse. The crowd started to hoot and holler, thinking it was part of the evening's entertainment.

"What happened to the lights?" Arvin shouted above the uproar. "Who turned out the lights?"

Harry shouted into Gillian's ear, "Where's our flashlight?"

She reached into her apron pocket and handed it to him.

"Good, now we can at least see." He moved the light around the room. But all he saw were the kids from the drama club.

Without electricity, the music also stopped, and the toadies could be heard loud and crystal clear.

Hop, thud, brush...hop, thud, brush...

"Wh...wh...what's that noise?" Gillian asked. "We need to find Mr. Chad, I'm scared!"

"Maybe this is part of the play. Maybe Mr. Chad

turned out the lights," Arvin said hopefully, although he didn't believe it himself.

"I don't think so," Harry said.

"Me either." Gillian stopped and listened. "What *is* that?"

The sound of the toadies' croaking grew louder and louder. The party crowd quieted down and listened too.

"It's coming from the back of the house," Harry said.

"You mean *they* are coming from the back of the house. Look!" Arvin pointed. The costumed party guests screamed and ran out the front door, as the toadies entered through the back.

"Are they t..t..t..toads?" Arvin stammered.

"They're not like any toads I've ever seen!" Harry shouted.

"They're huge! Bigger than huge! They're humongous!!!" Gillian screamed.

Hop, thud, brush...

"DO SOMETHING!!" Gillian screamed.

Arvin looked around in a panic. "We're the only ones left! Everyone else escaped! We can't get to the door! They've got us trapped!!"

Gillian flattened herself against the wall, as if that would somehow help. "There are so many of them... they're everywhere..."

Suddenly, they heard an electric sounding SIZZLE!

"Look!" Harry cried in amazement. "Look what happens when I shine the light on them." SIZZLE!

"Shining the light on their skin stops them!" Gillian almost cheered, but then saw something that made her gasp. "What are those things in the air?"

"Brooms. *Floating* brooms." Harry shined the light all around. "There's one behind each toad. The brooms are brushing away the toads' tracks!"

Arvin nodded tentatively toward the corner. "One broom is glowing!"

"We've got to find Mr. Chad!" Gillian hollered.

"I think we have," Harry said slowly. "That glowing broom is right behind that toad...and that toad is wearing a...cape and a...goatee!"

Chapter 7
Escape

"Aaahh!!!" Harry, Gillian and Arvin ran out the front door, but they never heard it slam. A floating broom held it open while the toadies passed through.

Hop, thud, brush...

The slow, heavy sounds picked up speed. The toadies moved quickly now, despite their bulky weight.

Hop, thud, brush...faster and faster...

"Run to the barn! HURRY!" Harry yelled. But he didn't have to, Gillian and Arvin were racing blurs.

Gillian swung her head around to see where the toadies were. Her shoe caught in the folds of her long dress. She tripped and fell to the ground. The swirl of party guests ran past her in all different directions. But the toadies didn't follow them. They only chased Harry, Gillian and Arvin!

"They're after US!" she cried. She jumped up, raised her long skirt above her knees, and ran like crazy toward the barn. The toadies were right behind her.

The huge, lumbering toadies and their brooms moved with amazing speed, and were just about to overtake Gillian...

"HARRY!" Gillian screamed into the night air. She had no idea where he was, because her eyes were fixed on the ugly toadie who was pointing his broom at her!

Then she heard it. SIZZLE! Out of nowhere, Harry's flashlight beam crackled on the toadie's slimy green skin. The toadie cowered, and its broom fell to the ground.

Just then, a car engine roared at the end of the long driveway. The squeaky passenger door opened and out climbed Mondo in his leather jacket and sunglasses. He slammed the door of his brother's car and swaggered down the driveway toward Harry.

"Hey, Hairball!" Mondo snarled. He was ready for vengeance.

"Oh, no! It's Mondo!" Harry turned and let his flashlight beam drop. The toadie lunged toward him.

"Harry!!!" Gillian grabbed the flashlight out of his hand and thrust it at the toadie.

SIZZLE!

Then she grabbed Harry's elbow and pulled him along. "Come on! Let's get to the barn!"

"Hey Hairball!" Mondo spit the words out. "I've got you now!"

"*You've* got me?" Harry hollered, running toward the barn with the toadies after him. "Take a number, Mondo!"

"Hurry! Get in here!" Arvin yelled as he held the barn door open for them. They ran the last stretch, and leapt inside the barn just as Arvin slammed the old rickety door in the toadies' faces.

"Whew! Made it!" Harry was panting hard.

"Harry, quick, slide that metal thing in so it locks." Gillian held the door shut with all her strength.

The metal bar clanked and Harry carefully stepped away from the door to make sure it held. Then he turned to Arvin and Gillian, "Is everybody okay?"

"Yeah, of course," Arvin nodded, trying hard to keep his bravado up, but he was obviously shaken.

Outside, strange wails from cows, horses and sheep filled the night air. But there were no animals at the deserted farm...

Chapter 8
The Hayloft

"Hey guys! Look, there are some old steps going up to the hayloft." Gillian took the creaking steps two at a time. "I see a window up there."

"O.K., you guard up there," Harry called out. "We'll guard down here."

Suddenly, there was a loud CRACK!

"Aaahh!!"

Harry jerked around, "Gillian!"

A rotten wood step gave way and Gillian's feet slid through the hole. She clung to the sides of the stairs, but was unable to hold on. She was slipping through, when Arvin appeared under the staircase.

"Gillian, put your feet on my hands," he said, as he grabbed her feet and straightened them out. He hoisted her up so she had traction. Then he gave her a big push, and she was able to lift herself out of the hole and swing her legs onto the next step, which held her weight.

She stood up, brushed off the dust, and peered down through the hole. In a small voice she said, "Thanks for your help, Arvin..." But he was already gone.

She stood there, looking through the hole for a moment. Then she turned and made her way up the rickety steps to the top. She walked carefully along the hayloft boards toward the far end.

There was a dark pocket in the corner that gave her the chills. Was something hidden in the shadows? Yes, she could feel it. But what is it? Could it be a toadie?

She waited for something in the shadowy spot to move or make a noise, but nothing did. Her eyes stayed focused on it, adjusting to the darkness. Slowly, she crept across the loft toward the window. Tiny slivers of moonlight shone through the cracks in its wooden shutter. She reached the window, felt for its hook and opened it. The wooden shutter swung back, and moonlight seeped in. It flickered over the dark spot just enough to let her see what was hidden there.

In the dim light, she could see it wasn't a toadie. It was something square, like a box, covered in grimy dirt. She quickly knelt down next to it and brushed off the top. It was an old cedar chest. Very, very old. She carefully checked to see if it was locked. It wasn't. She worked the rusty metal hinges back and forth until she could finally ease the lid open. The hinges squeaked horribly.

"What's going on up there?" Harry called out. But Gillian didn't answer.

"Ohhh," she cooed to herself. "Look at all these clothes. They're beautiful and so old. This long dress and this apron and this bonnet, they're.... Oh, my gosh! They look just like the costume I'm wearing! They must belong to the Goodwife of Hamstead Farm!"

She felt something small and hard buried in the bottom of the chest. She reached in and pulled out—a salt shaker!

"Ouch!" An electric spark shocked her hand. She dropped the shaker and salt spilled from it. What? An electric current—from a salt shaker??

"Harry! Arvin! Come up here!" she called. "I found something."

"Just a minute!" Harry was more concerned about the toadies on the other side of the barn door.

Gillian dug deeper into the chest and found a small book. Its pages were fragile and yellow. It looked like a very old diary. When she opened it, a paper fell out. Gently, she unfolded it and began to read.

October 31, 1824

To Thee:

They call me the Goodwife
of Hamstead Farm.
I'm also the Good Witch
who battles harm.

The Evil Witch is captive
in the gnarled oak tree.
One day she will try to
outwit my decree.

She will capture three
souls to break the spell,
and substitute them in
her wooden cell.

To halt her trickery...

Hop, thud, brush...

Gillian froze. "Who's there?" Her voice was barely a whisper. "Harry? Arvin? Where are you?"

Hop, thud, brush...

"Harry! Arvin!" Gillian hid behind the cedar chest. In the stream of moonlight from the barn window, Gillian saw it. This time she was sure. It was—a toadie!

"Aaahh!!" she screamed. "How...how did you get in?"

The toadie pointed the bristles of its suspended broom at Gillian. Her eyes grew wide and she was unable to move. WHOOSH! In a flash of green light, Gillian was vaporized and sucked into the broomstick.

"Aaahh!" Gillian's voice gurgled and faded away. The putrid green mist covered the toadie. When it cleared, the toadie was wearing a miniature version of Gillian's apron and bonnet. Its broom now glowed.

Harry and Arvin heard Gillian's scream and ran up the old, creaky stairs to the hayloft, narrowly missing the broken step. "Gillian! Gillian!"

But there was no response.

When he reached the top, Harry shined his flashlight on the first thing he saw—the glowing broom. The broom immediately dropped onto the hay. The toadie tried to grab it, but was stopped by the light sizzling on its slimy green skin.

"The toadie can't get the broom as long as you shine your flashlight on it!" Arvin exclaimed.

"That's not a broom," Harry said sadly. "That's Gillian."

Chapter 9
Mondo's Turn

Outside the barn, Mondo slid a pencil flashlight from behind his ear and shined it in the toadies' eyes—just to irritate them. "So what's with the slimy green costumes? You are uuugly!" He laughed obnoxiously as he jerked the light back and forth over the toadies, unaware that it was saving him.

A crow cawed in the distance. Flapping wings approached, then faded away. Suddenly, a wild wind hissed around the barn. Branches pounded against the farmhouse windows. Doors rattled on their hinges.

"What's going on?" Mondo called out in a panic. He pounded on the barn door. "Hey, you guys, open up! Come on, open the door!"

Wails from cows, horses and sheep filled the creepy night air.

"I..I..I don't get it." Mondo was really scared now.

"There aren't any animals here...."

A toadie hopped behind Mondo. A suspended broom swept away its tracks. As the toadie came closer, the farm animals' moans grew louder and more distressed.

Hop, thud, brush...

"Who's out there?" Mondo looked into the black night. "What's going on?" His snarly voice was now a soft whimper. "Hey guys? Let me in the barn. Hey, Hairball!...Hairball!....Harry?"

The low rumbling turned into croaks. More and more toadies appeared out of the darkness. They surrounded Mondo on three sides and backed him up against the barn door. "Aaahh!" He covered his face with his hands and dropped the flashlight.

Immediately, a toadie pointed its broom bristles at Mondo. WHOOSH!! In a flash of green light, he was vaporized.

Aaahh!" Mondo's gurgling voice sounded far way, then it disappeared altogether as he was sucked into the broom.

The toadie now wore a miniature version of Mondo's leather jacket and sunglasses. Its broom now glowed.

Chapter 10
Toadies in the Barn

Harry and Arvin crouched in the hayloft. Through the window, they saw everything.

At the same time, they had to keep their eyes on the hideous toadie wearing Gillian's costume, and make sure the flashlight beam kept it at bay.

Whatever was going to happen next, inside or outside, they were going to be ready.

A hollow wind rose out of the field. Unintelligible voices whispered in the distance. The whispers turned into eerie wails.

Hop, thud, brush...

The barn door creaked opened. Arvin's eyes widened. "I thought it was locked!"

"It was," Harry whispered. "We've got to get out

of here." He looked around. The loft window was the only way. "Come on, you go first." Harry handed the flashlight to Arvin and lifted him up to the high window ledge.

Thump, thump, thump...

"They're coming up the steps!" Arvin whipped around and dropped the flashlight in his excitement. Immediately, the Gillian toadie lunged for the flashlight and broom!

Harry dumped Arvin on the floor, rolled across the boards, and scooped up the flashlight mid-stream.

"Arvin, look out!" At the top of the stairs, leading the rest of the toadies, was the biggest, greenest, meanest toadie of them all. "It's pointing its broom at you!"

Arvin quickly dove out of the line of fire. The green light from the broom ricocheted off the walls with a high, piercing screech.

"Wow! That was close!" Harry reached forward to pick up Gillian's broom. But the big toadie quickly pointed its bristles in Harry's direction. A burst of green light shot out.

The light ricocheted off the walls. Harry dove out of the way and the beam hit an old bale of hay behind him. It sizzled into smoking ashes.

Just then, a church bell rang out. The big toadie stopped and listened. It turned robotically and thudded down the steps and out of the barn. All the other toadies followed him.

Hop, thud, brush...hop, thud, brush...

Harry and Arvin ran to the window. All the toadies hopped across the field toward the gnarly old tree.

"We've still got Gillian's broom!" Arvin proclaimed.

Harry looked at it sadly. "But how do we get her *out* of the broom?"

Chapter 11
The Spell

"How do we get them all back? How do we get Gillian, Mr. Chad and Mondo out of the brooms?" Harry asked.

Arvin watched out the window as the toadies hopped across the field. He shook his head sadly. "I don't think we can..."

Just then, moonlight flickered through the window, drawing their attention to the ancient chest. "Look!" Harry ran to the dark corner and knelt down. "This is what Gillian found." He started to open the chest, when he saw the paper lying near it. He picked it up and read aloud:

> October 31, 1824
>
> To Thee:
>
> They call me the Goodwife
> of Hamstead Farm.

I'm also the Good Witch
who battles harm.

The Evil Witch is captive
in the gnarled oak tree.
One day she will try to
outwit my decree.

She will capture three souls
to break the spell,
and substitute them in
her wooden cell.

To halt her trickery,
you have only until midnight.
Conjure me with this spell.
Say it loud, say it right.

Arvin grabbed the paper from Harry and looked at the spell written at the bottom of the page. "Wow! Mr. Chad's play really was true."

"It says three souls." Harry looked at the toadie's glowing broom. "And we've still got Gillian."

"If we don't get her out of this broom by midnight, she could stay in there forever!" Arvin shouted.

"The letter says the gnarled oak tree. We don't have much time. We'll have to take our bikes." Harry was already on his way down the steps, Arvin followed.

"Ride bikes through the field?" Arvin wasn't convinced.

"It's the fastest way." Harry turned and handed the paper to Arvin. "You take the spell, I'll take Gillian's broom."

They ran out the door and around the corner of the barn where their bikes were parked. Harry grabbed his handlebars, then stopped. "Somebody poked a hole in my tire!"

"Mondo!" Arvin said in disgust.

"You ride your bike and take the spell," Harry said. "I'll run with the broom. Go!"

Arvin didn't say a word, he just hopped on his bike and peddled as fast as he could over the hard, bumpy field. Several times his wheels skidded and spun backwards, throwing him hard on the dirt. But each time he got right back up and peddled on.

When Arvin got near the gnarled old tree, he stopped and laid his bike down in a crevice so it couldn't be seen. Then he crawled on his stomach, moving as close as he could to the tree without alerting the toadies. He held the spell tightly in his hand.

The toadies sat inside the charred circle surrounding the gnarled oak tree. Their chanting filled the air, but Arvin couldn't understand any of it.

Suddenly, a huge explosion rocked the ground and the toadies scattered. As the smoke cleared, the toadies carefully made their way back to the circle where the Evil Witch now stood.

"As the midnight hour approaches, we must act

quickly," the Evil Witch said. "Come, my little toadies. Bring forth the jealous brooms."

The toadie wearing Mr. Chad's black cape and goatee presented its broom to the Evil Witch. As she took the glowing broom and held it above her head, the toadie watched proudly.

The Evil Witch chanted, "Toona Toona Da Boo." Then she tapped the broom three times. With a loud WHOOSH! Mr. Chad was vaporized into the tree. The toadies croaked gleefully, and the witch's fingers turned from tree branches into flesh.

The Evil Witch took the second glowing broom from the toadie wearing Mondo's leather jacket and sunglasses. The toadie sat proudly in front of her.

"Toona Toona, Da Boo." The Evil Witch tapped the Mondo broom three times. Another loud WHOOSH! and Mondo was vaporized into the tree. The toadies rocked back and forth with excitement, and the Evil Witch's skin was no longer covered in bark.

"Three jealous brooms will set me free!" The Evil Witch cackled wildly. "Now, for the last one." She paused, but the Gillian toadie did not come forth. "Where is the last glowing broom?" she screeched.

The toadies only twitched and croaked and looked toward the Gillian toadie cowering in the woods.

"Go find the broom!" The Evil Witch shouted angrily at the toadie. "There's not much time! GO!"

Just then, they heard rustling in the field. The Evil Witch turned her black, smoldering eyes toward the sound. The toadies turned too.

There stood Arvin with the spell tightly gripped in his hands. With a shaky voice, he read:

"Goodwife of Hamstead Farm,
come release us from this harm.
Teepor Van Tampor."

Thunder crackled and lightning bolts flickered in the sky. Then, a burst of white, sparkly smoke covered the age-old circle of salt.

"Hello Evil Sister," the Goodwife said from behind the clearing smoke.

"Who conjured you?" shrieked the Evil Witch, stepping back.

"Someone who wants you back in the tree," the Goodwife said smoothly, moving nearer to her sister.

"No! No more..." the Evil Witch screamed. She tried to move away, but her feet were planted in the ground like a tree trunk.

The Evil Witch lifted her hands toward the Goodwife, but as soon as she did, her fingers turned back into thin, wispy branches. Her skin hardened into tree bark.

"Aaahh!!" the Evil Witch bellowed.

The Goodwife threw out beams of powerful light that swallowed up each of the three toadies, and finally, the Evil Witch. With one WHOOSH after another, they were vaporized into the tree.

As quickly as it came, the fiery light disappeared. It left smoldering patches in the grass where the Evil Witch and the toadies used to be.

When the smoke settled, two lifeless brown brooms laid on the ground in front of the gnarled old tree. Mr. Chad and Mondo stood in front of them, both were back to their normal selves.

"Only fifteen seconds until midnight," Arvin said. "Where's Harry with that broom?"

Chapter 12
Midnight

Mr. Chad pointed into the distance. They could see Harry coming toward them, but he was still too far away to make it by midnight. He huffed and puffed as he ran over the bumpy field with the Gillian broom under his arm.

"Harry! Harry, you've got to hurry!" Arvin cried out.

"I'm coming. I'm coming," Harry panted.

"Hurry up! You don't have any time!" Arvin shouted.

"I'll make it." Harry gasped. "Don't worry, I'll make it!"

Arvin watched him sadly. He was too far away, and he was Gillian's only hope.

"He's going to have to throw it," Mondo said, almost to himself. Both Mr. Chad and Arvin turned and looked at Mondo as if he was a genius. Mondo smiled, then stood up straight and shouted, "Come on Harry, throw it! You can do it!"

"Throw that stick, Harry!" Arvin hollered.

"I'm going to, going to...make it!" Harry barely got the words out, he was so out of breath.

Arvin shook his head. "He's not listening," he said sadly. "It's over."

Mondo looked at Arvin, then at Harry. He cupped his hands around his mouth and shouted at the top of his lungs, "You're Gillian's only chance! THROW THAT JAVELIN!!"

Harry looked at his watch, then at the broom. He closed his eyes briefly, then opened them. With all of his strength, he threw the broom, like a javelin, toward the tree. It soared through the night sky like a radar honing in on its target.

The church bell began to ring in the distance. Each CLANG closed in on midnight. Just as the Goodwife was beginning to fade away, the Gillian broom landed at her feet. The Goodwife turned and smiled. With all the power she had left, she squeezed a beam of light from her hands and flooded it over the broom.

The light sparkled on the broom, clouding it with smoke. Then a soft breeze cleared the air.

There stood Gillian.

The Goodwife turned to Gillian and smiled. They were dressed alike. "Remember Gillian, you are the *good* sister, not the jealous sister."

Gillian nodded. "I'll remember."

And with that, the Goodwife disappeared, along with the circle of salt. The knothole in the gnarled old tree was empty. The toadies were simply toads again, and they hopped into the woods.

Mr. Chad, Gillian, Mondo, Arvin and Harry all walked silently through the field toward the farmhouse. Everything was the same again, except that Mondo was walking with them instead of chasing after them.

And of course, Arvin couldn't keep quiet for long. He slapped Harry on the back. "So, you did just like I taught you, Harry old boy. You closed your eyes, and you imagined that javelin soaring through the air..."

"Stick," Harry said. "It wasn't a javelin, Arvin, it was a stick–a Toadie's broomstick.

THE END

Are you ready to star in your own Movie for the Ear?

(Insert applause here.)

Come in.

(Door creaking open.)

Holly will tell you how to get started.

Create Your Own
Movie for the Ear®

Hello, I'm Holly!

We may have already met in some of the other Creepers Mysteries. But if you're new here, let me show you around.

This way, follow me...

Okay. If you think that was a short trip, you're right. Because you can create a Movie for the Ear anywhere. Here's what you need:

- You
- Your Toadies script
- Friends or family members
- Sound effects that you create

A Movie for the Ear® is all about sound. You act out your part with your voice. You read the lines the way your character would say them. Next, you can have fun creating sound effects. You can even add music!

Here's how to get started:

1. Cast the Roles

Toadies is full of fun characters.

You can read the entire script by yourself, or you can divide the roles with one or two other people. I do that all the time when I'm rehearsing for a part.

For a full Movies for the Ear® production, cast your classmates, friends, or family in the roles. Remember, actors can play more than one part. They just have to use a different voice for each character. You'll get the hang of it.

2. Rehearse

Your director will organize and oversee your rehearsals. Rehearsing means that you and your fellow actors will read your lines over and over again, until you're very familiar with them.

Make sure everyone is comfortable with their lines before you start to add sound effects or music.

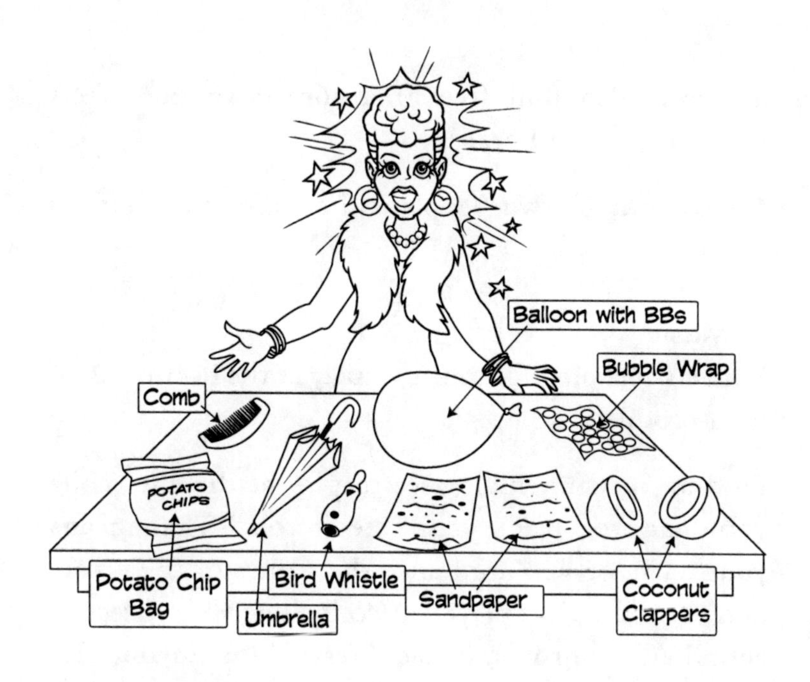

3. Sound Effects (SFX)

Go through the script and note the items labeled "SFX." That stands for Sound Effects. Mark a few that you would like to try. You can even add new sound effects wherever you would like them. Next, you get to find creative ways to make the sounds.

Here are some examples:

Footsteps: Shoes on a wood bread board
Thunder: Balloon with BBs inside, roll slowly
Fire: Crinkle a cellophane potato chip bag

Gather all the items you will need to create your sounds in one place. This way you can move easily from one sound to the next during your production.

You can also find free pre-recorded sound effects online or at your library.

Choose one or two people to be your sound effects artists.

4. Music

Find a short piece of music to play at the beginning of your production.

Find an instrumental piece to play at the end while your narrator reads your "credit roll." That means your narrator will announce the names of the actors and the parts they played. Also include your director, sound effects artists, music director, and anyone else who worked on your production.

If you would like, you can play other short pieces of music at key points in your Movie for the Ear.

5. Make a Poster

Download the poster template from the website, www.creepersmysteries.com. Customize it for your own production, and use it to invite your audience.

I know you'll have a blast starring in your own Movie for the Ear! Break a leg! (That's Hollywood talk for "good luck!")

—Holly

CREEPERS® Mysteries

Toadies

Movie for the Ear Script

By Connie Kingrey Anderson

Movies for the Ear®

CREEPERS® Mysteries
Toadies
Cast & Crew

Production Company ______________________________

Director ______________________________

Ebeneezer Stump/Narrator ______________________________

Harry ______________________________

Gillian ______________________________

Arvin ______________________________

Mondo ______________________________

Mr. Chad, the Drama Teacher ______________________________

Goodwife of Hamstead Farm ______________________________

Husband of Hamstead Farm ______________________________

The Evil Witch ______________________________

Sound Effects Artist #1 ______________________________

Sound Effects Artist #2 ______________________________

Music Director ______________________________

CREEPERS® Mysteries
Toadies
Movie for the Ear Script

MUSIC: CREEPERS THEME SONG

SFX: FOOTSTEPS. KEY IN THE DOOR LOCK. LOCK TURNING. DOOR CREAKING OPEN.

EBENEEZER: Hello, come in. I'm Ebeneezer Stump. And you are? Oh, I see. Hmmm... You are here for a Creepers Mystery.

SFX: LOW, RUMBLING TOADS CROAKING. BROOMS BRUSHING.

EBENEEZER: Have you ever been in a dark woods with just the trees and the toads? Have you ever been afraid of what a toadie can do in the dark? (STING) Get ready for this episode of Creepers Mysteries. Here it comes ...*Toadies.*

ACT I, Scene 1

SFX: SCHOOL LOCKERS BEING SHUT, KIDS TALKING.

HARRY: Arvin, do you know what a toadie is?

ARVIN: Well of course, doesn't everybody?

HARRY: You have no idea, do you?

ARVIN: None.

HARRY: Say there's a big bully. Well, all the guys that hang around him, the junior bullies, they aren't bullies at all. They just do what the big bully says. So they're toadies.

ARVIN: Toadies, huh?

HARRY: Yeah.

ARVIN: What if a guy is just a junior bully? He thinks he's a big bully, but there's no way.

HARRY: Then he's still a toadie.

ARVIN: Like Mondo over there?

HARRY: Mondo? Definitely a toadie.

MONDO: Ooooh! Look at this!

SFX: PAPER CRINKLING

GILLIAN: Hey, give it back! Mondo! Give it back!

MONDO: Wow! This drawing is so cool, Gillian, I could almost puke!

GILLIAN: Mondo! Do you mind? Mondo! Give it here!

MONDO: (laughing) I better put this garbage in the garbage. You don't want to be a litter bug, Gillian.

GILLIAN: Mondo! Don't you dare put my drawing in the garbage! MONDOOOOOO!!!

ARVIN: Harry, we better help your sister.

HARRY: Yeah, let's go.

SFX: BELL RINGS

MONDO: Oh, saved by the bell. Here's your stupid drawing, Gillian. What do I want with it anyway.

MUSIC: JEALOUSY PANG

SFX: FOOTSTEPS MOVING down the hallway.

ARVIN: Look at him hop!

HARRY: He's just jealous because he can't draw. Is your picture okay Gillian?

GILLIAN: Yeah, I guess. It's a little wrinkled, but he didn't wreck it too much.

ARVIN: What is it?

GILLIAN: It's a drawing of how to decorate the old Hamstead Farm for the Halloween Party.

ARVIN: The Drama Club's Halloween Party?

GILLIAN: Yeah. I drew everything just where I think it should go. See, we can put pumpkins right along the doorway, and haystacks over here.

ARVIN: What's that thing?

GILLIAN: It's a prickly old vine we're going to wind up the staircase.

HARRY: Spooky.

GILLIAN: I just hope Mr. Chad picks me to be the decorating chairperson.

HARRY: With that drawing? Of course he will. Come on, you guys. We better get to the Drama Club meeting.

ARVIN: It's in Mr. Chad's classroom.

GILLIAN: I just hope Mondo's not there.

HARRY & ARVIN: Mondo? He's a toadie.

GILLIAN: What's a toadie?

ACT I, Scene 2

MUSIC: TRANSITION

SFX: DOOR OPENING. CROWD OF KIDS TALKING.

MR. CHAD: Welcome, come on in and have a seat. We're just getting started.

SFX: DESKS MOVING, TALKING

MR. CHAD: Now, before we assign committees for the Halloween party, we're going to read through the play that the Drama Club will be performing. It's just a little something I wrote. Although, I know I'm not as talented a writer as your previous drama teacher, Mr. Goldman.

MUSIC: JEALOUSY PANG

MR. CHAD: I'm sure you all know that Mr. Goldman has his play on Broadway and lots of money in his pocket....

ARVIN: (whispering to Harry) Not too jealous, is he?

HARRY: Really.

GILLIAN: You guys, SHHHH!

MR. CHAD: I'm sorry, I got carried away. Now, you all know the local legend of Hamstead Farm, which is where we'll be having our Halloween party. So, regardless of whether or not you believe the legend, it makes a great play for Halloween.

As the actors read through the play, the rest of you close your eyes. Pretend that you are at Hamstead Farm that very Halloween night in 1824. Imagine that you hear all the sounds—the hissing wind, the howling of wolves...and the voices of witches. Let's begin.

SFX: WAVY "IMAGINATION" MUSIC/SOUND

MR. CHAD: (narrating) Mr. Chad's Halloween play, The Legend of Hamstead Farm.

It's All Hallow's Eve in 1824. The sky is ominous. Dark clouds pass over the moon.

SFX: CROWS CALL. FLAPPING WINGS swoop down, then fade into the distance.

MR. CHAD: (narrating) A stone farmhouse and barn can be seen in the flicker of moonlight. The fields are full of withered and dead cornstalks. Far off in the distance, over gently rolling hills, is a gloomy woods.

What's that? Are there eyes watching from the woods? Or are those just blinking shadows?

SFX: WOLVES HOWL. WIND HISSES. BRANCHES BEAT against windows. DOORS RATTLE on hinges.

MR. CHAD: (narrating) A sudden wind hisses around the farmhouse, beating branches against the windows and rattling doors on their hinges. It's not a safe night for man or beast...or witch.

A single lantern glows in the side window of the stone farmhouse. Through the drawn curtain, we see shadows of a man and a woman sitting at a table. In the barn, the animals know there is danger in the air.

SFX: Farm ANIMALS WAILING

HUSBAND: But, my Goodwife, the cows do not give milk, the hens have stopped laying eggs, and the corn has all withered in the field.

GOODWIFE: Rest assured, dear husband. Things will soon be better.

HUSBAND: You are truly a good and hopeful wife. But our efforts are in vain. Listen to the animals wail.

SFX: Farm ANIMALS WAILING

GOODWIFE: We have been cursed by my sister, the Evil Witch. Go to bed now and rest, husband. When the cock crows in the morning, all will be well again.

MR. CHAD: (narrating) By the moon's glow, a large toadie hops along the dirt path toward the barn. A floating broom follows the toadie, sweeping away its tracks.

SFX: HOP, THUD, BRUSH

MR. CHAD: (narrating) Suddenly, the Goodwife appears. She carries a lantern and a shaker of salt. She speaks to the toadie.

GOODWIFE: Good evening, Evil Witch. I see you are disguised as one of your toadies.

MR. CHAD: (narrating) The toadie stops. The floating broom falls to the ground.

SFX: BROOM HITS THE GROUND

MR. CHAD: (Narrating) The Goodwife throws salt on the toadie. Then she flashes the lantern toward it. The light sizzles on the toadie's skin.

SFX: SIZZLE

GOODWIFE: Ride in my apron, toadie, across the field to the gnarled oak tree.

SFX: MAGICAL SOUND

GOODWIFE: Now, watch as I pour a circle of salt around the tree. Inside you go.

MR. CHAD: (narrating) In the midst of a sickening green glow, the toadie becomes a young woman. She is dressed all in black. She is the Evil Witch.

EVIL WITCH: Hello sister. You are quite convincing in your role as the Goodwife of Hamstead Farm. Doesn't your husband know you are a witch just like me?

GOODWIFE: A witch, yes. But not like you. Our father always knew you would use your powers for evil, and I would use my powers for good.

EVIL WITCH: And because of that, father left you Hamstead Farm! It should have been mine!

MUSIC: JEALOUSY PANGS

EVIL WITCH: See this small wooden farmhouse I hold in my hand? It's Hamstead Farm. (wicked laughter)

SFX: Dry WOOD CATCHING FIRE and CRACKLING.

EVIL WITCH: It was Hamstead Farm!

GOODWIFE: Stop! It is now my turn to stop the burn. Fire, be gone!

SFX: TWINKLING OF A "SPELL." THE FIRE IS PUT OUT.

EVIL WITCH: You aren't going to let me have any fun, are you?

GOODWIFE: Why let your jealousy destroy the very farm you wanted?

EVIL WITCH: Because my jealousy rules! If I can't have Hamstead Farm, then neither will you!

MUSIC: JEALOUSY PANG

GOODWIFE: Your evil jealousy has no power here.

MR. CHAD: (narrating) The Evil Witch is furious. Her body sizzles and smoke rises from beneath her black robe.

EVIL WITCH: Jealousy fuels my evil! It empowers me! It will destroy Hamstead Farm and those in it!

MR. CHAD: (narrating) The Evil Witch lunges toward the Goodwife. But when she crosses the salt circle, she is flung back against the tree with a forceful gust, as if hit by an electrical current.

EVIL WITCH: Aaahh!

MUSIC: CHORAL

GOODWIFE: This spell shall imprison your jealous spirit in the tree. This poisonous vine shall be the lock and key.

MR. CHAD: (narrating) The Evil Witch melts into the tree.

EVIL WITCH: Aaahh!

SFX: SUCKING NOISE

GOODWIFE: Goodbye, jealous sister. Good riddance, Evil Witch.

MUSIC: CHORAL MUSIC swells, then stops.

MR. CHAD: (narrating) The Goodwife turns and walks through the field. In a knothole in the craggy bark, there is one yellow, evil eye watching the Goodwife as she disappears into the distance.

MUSIC: EERIE MUSIC up and out

MR. CHAD: O.K., Drama Club, here are the committees

for the Halloween Party. Decorating Committee: Harry is the Chairperson.....

GILLIAN: Harry?

MUSIC: JEALOUSY PANG

ACT 1, Scene 3

EBENEEZER: Harry is on the athletic field practicing his javelin throw. But instead of a javelin, he's actually using a long stick that looks like a broom handle. Arvin stands nearby. Mondo watches from the sidelines, wearing his older brother's leather jacket so he'll look tough. But he's just short and squatty, kind of like a toad...

MONDO: Hey Hairball! I heard you choked at the track meet! Did it sound like this, Hairball? (cough, cough, then laughter)

ARVIN: Harry, don't listen to Mondo, he's a dweeb. He's just jealous that's all. (calling out) Hey Mondo, I didn't even see you at the track meet, so shut up!

MONDO: Harry, the Hairball. Choke, Choke! (laughter).

ARVIN: What a dweeb. (shift) So, Harry. What are you doing out here on the practice field on a Saturday? Do you see anybody else out here throwing a stick?

HARRY: Javelin.

ARVIN: Javelin. Not only is it Saturday, it's Halloween. The party's tonight. We've got stuff to do.

HARRY: After I choked at last week's track meet, I've got to practice. Just one more throw and then we'll go.

ARVIN: Alright, close your eyes.

HARRY: What? (sarcastically) Arvin, looking where I'm throwing could be the key to this whole thing.

ARVIN: You're visualizing. All the big athletes do it. Statistics show..."

HARRY: Alright, alright already, they're closed.

ARVIN: Now, see yourself throwing the stick.

HARRY: Javelin.

ARVIN: Javelin. Watch it soaring through the air. Do you see it?

HARRY: No. My eyes are closed.

ARVIN: You've got to really concentrate. Try again. There it goes, flying through the air.

HARRY: Oh, there it is, yeah I can see it now.

ARVIN: Okay, don't lose that image. Slowly open your eyes and throw that stick.

HARRY: Javelin.

ARVIN: Javelin. Are you ready?

HARRY: Yeah.

ARVIN: Go for it!

MONDO: HAAAAAIRBALL!

HARRY: Ugh! Oh no....

ARVIN: Uh oh. Harry, it's soaring in the wrong direction. It's headed straight toward Mondo!

MONDO: Aaaaaaaaahhhhh!!!

HARRY: I had my eyes closed. Mondo moved in front of me!

ARVIN: OOOOHH! Oh! Mondo ducked just in the nick of time.

EBENEEZER: Mondo slowly stood up. He scrunched his angry red face and balled up his fists. Then he grabbed his bike and pounded it upright on the pavement.

HARRY: Come on! Let's get out of here.

ARVIN: Our bikes are on the other side of the fence.

HARRY: We've got to make a run for it. Hurry! Hurry!

MUSIC: CHASE MUSIC

ARVIN: Hurry up! Hurry up! He's coming right at us! He's really snorting!

HARRY: I'm trying, I'm trying.

ARVIN: We can't make it. We're going to be history.

MR. CHAD: (calling out) Mondo! Mondo, could you help me load the party supplies?

SFX: BIKE BRAKES SQUEAK, TIRES SKID.

MONDO: Uh, sure Mr. Chad.

ARVIN: Wow! Saved by the drama teacher!

EBENEEZER: Little did Arvin and Harry know that it would soon be the drama teacher who would need to be saved...

SFX: HOP, THUD, BRUSH

MUSIC: TRANSITION

ACT II, Scene 1

EBENEEZER: Harry and Arvin arrive at Hamstead Farm ready to decorate. They park their bikes, then carry their sacks through the field to the woods beyond. They find a gnarled old oak tree with a large, prickly vine around it. They start to gather fall leaves.

SFX: LOW CROAKS

ARVIN: Hey, there's Gillian coming through the field. She doesn't look too happy.

HARRY: (calling out cheerfully) Hey Gillian, we found some great decorations for you! Check out this vine!

EBENEEZER: But Gillian was having none of it. She stomped toward them with an angry look on her face.

ARVIN: (innocently) What's the matter Gillian?

GILLIAN: (ignoring Arvin) Harry, why did Mr. Chad pick you for the decorating chairperson? It should have been me! I did all this work.

HARRY: I'm sorry, Gillian. I think he just picked me because I'm tall. I can put the decorations up high.

GILLIAN: Sure. Why do you always get everything, Harry? Everything is always Harry, Harry, Harry!

MUSIC: JEALOUSY PANG

EBENEEZER: From behind Gillian's head, there is a faint glow of a yellow eye peering out of the tree's knothole. A toad hops on Gillian's tennis shoe. She kicks her foot and the toad goes flying. She stomps back toward the farmhouse.

HARRY: Boy, she was really mad.

ARVIN: (under his breath) Jealous.

HARRY: We'll decorate everything just like her drawing.

That should make her happy. Look, here's the prickly vine.

ARVIN: Hey, did it just get dark really fast?

HARRY: Yeah, it did. We better hurry.

EBENEEZER: A toad hops on Arvin's shoe. He shakes his foot to get it off.

ARVIN: I have a feeling we're not alone.

EBENEEZER: Out of the darkness a group of toads appear. They stare at Arvin with beady eyes. They don't move. They barely blink. Arvin freezes.

ARVIN: (scared) What's with all these toads all of a sudden?

EBENEEZER: The toads surround them both now, their beady eyes almost floating in the dark.

HARRY: (whispering) This is really weird. Let's get our decorations and get out of here.

ARVIN: Yeah!

HARRY: This vine is too thick. We need a knife.

SFX: HOWLING WIND, TOADS CROAKING

MUSIC: SUSPENSEFUL

EBENEEZER: The toads move toward Harry and Arvin, closer and closer.

MR. CHAD: (calling out) Harry? Arvin? Are you out there?

ARVIN: Whew! It's Mr. Chad. (calling out) Yeah, we're here! We're over here.

SFX: FOOTSTEPS CRUNCH in dry grass.

EBENEEZER: Mr. Chad is already in his costume. He is dressed as Shakespeare, with a cape and goatee. As he comes nearer, the toadies retreat into the woods.

MR. CHAD: (startled) Oh! There you are. Excuse me for stepping on your foot, Arvin.

ARVIN: That wasn't my foot.

EBENEEZER: Arvin looks at the patches of moving grass and leaves. He knows exactly what Mr. Chad stepped on.

HARRY: We want to wrap this vine around the staircase. But we need a knife to cut it.

MR. CHAD: I've got a pocket knife. Why don't you go back and get started with the other decorations. I'll bring the vine.

HARRY: O.K. Thanks Mr. Chad. (shift) Hey! Wait up Arvin!

SFX: RUNNING THROUGH DRY FIELDS.

HARRY: (to Arvin) Do you think Mr. Chad will be okay out there alone?

ARVIN: Of course, he's a teacher.

ACT II, Scene 2

MUSIC: TRANSITIONAL, FOREBODING.

MR. CHAD: (to himself) This vine is really tough. Ugh!

SFX: SAWING ON VINE

MR. CHAD: (to himself) What am I doing out here, in the middle of nowhere, sticking myself with this prickly vine...while Mr. Goldman is sitting in a

Broadway theatre watching his own play... Ouch! This vine is sharp... Why couldn't my play be on Broadway? It's not fair. Why does Mr. Goldman get all the breaks, and not me?

MUSIC: JEALOUSY PANG

EBENEEZER: The yellow evil eye in the knothole glows. It whirls in its socket, straining to see beyond the tight hole. It watches every move Mr. Chad makes. The evil eye grows brighter, then fades. It glows more brightly still, before fading again. This continues back and forth, glowing and dimming, each time Mr. Chad saws on the vine.

MR. CHAD: (huffing and puffing) This is no ordinary vine. One more try and I'm giving up.

EBENEEZER: He takes a deep breath, and with everything he can muster, plunges the knife into the vine. This time he punctures it.

SFX: HIGH PITCHED SOUND, MIST SPRAYING

MR. CHAD: (coughing) What's this mist? It's...oh no!

MUSIC: EVIL AND FOREBODING

EBENEEZER: A green mist is released from the vine. It smokes and curls around Mr. Chad's head, then swirls around his body until it covers him. When the mist clears, Mr. Chad is no longer there.

MUSIC: STING

MUSIC: VINE UNWINDING

EBENEEZER: Slowly, the vine releases its hold and peels away from the gnarly old tree. The yellow evil eye in the knothole blinks. Then a second eye appears. The bark begins to bubble and roll in small waves, forming the face of a woman–no of a witch–pushing her way out.

SFX: GROANING, STRETCHING SOUNDS

EVIL WITCH: Aaahhh!

Act II, Scene 3

EBENEEZER: Finally, the Evil Witch breaks out of the tree! Her dark robe is the same, but the skin under it is covered with bark. Her fingers are wispy branches. Her grotesque face is gnarled, rough and pocked with knotholes. The only human thing about her is her evil yellow eyes.

She starts toward the farmhouse, placing one stump-like leg in front of the other. Suddenly, she is pushed back against the tree, as if hit by electric current.

SFX: ELECTRICAL SIZZLING

EVIL WITCH: Aaahh!

EBENEEZER: A thin line of fire sizzles around the tree, recreating the age-old circle of salt placed there by the Goodwife of Hamstead Farm.

EVIL WITCH: (Howling in frustration) Removing the vine removed only part of the curse! (shift) But look, the woods are sprinkled with bright beady eyes and familiar shadows.

SFX: CROAKS

EVIL WITCH: I have summoned you, my loyal toadies, to break the curse which has held me prisoner in this tree for hundreds of years.

SFX: RUSTLING OF DEAD LEAVES.

EVIL WITCH: First, I will drop three branches from this tree. When they hit the ground, small brooms they will be.

SFX: WHOOSH, DROP, MAGICAL STING

EVIL WITCH: Now, toadies, take these brooms. Use them as wands to ZAP three jealous souls. Put them in the tree to set me free. Put them in the tree instead of me.

SFX: RUSTLING OF DEAD LEAVES.

EVIL WITCH: Toadies, remember: Deliver them by midnight. And beware of the light.

EBENEEZER: As clouds pass in front of the moon, the toadies hop through the dry woods. In the distance, the lights of Hamstead Farm glow.

MUSIC: TRANSITIONAL

ACT III, Scene 1

EBENEEZER: Harry and Arvin are at the Halloween party in the farmhouse. They are decked out in their pirate costumes, waiting for Gillian to arrive.

MUSIC: DANCE MUSIC

ARVIN: The decorations turned out pretty well, don't you think?

HARRY: Yeah. I sure hope Gillian likes them.

ARVIN: She will. She must be putting on her costume. What's she wearing?

HARRY: A long dress, an apron, and an old-fashioned bonnet. She's the Goodwife of Hamstead Farm.

SFX: HOP, THUD, BRUSH...(Low in the background)

MUSIC: OMINOUS

ARVIN: Hey, here comes Gillian.

GILLIAN: (frantic) Where's Mr. Chad? It's time to start the play!

HARRY: Last time I saw him he was in the woods cutting the vine.

ARVIN: He never brought that vine. Maybe he never came back.

SFX: TOADS CROAKING

GILLIAN: What if something happened to him out there?

SFX: HOP, THUD, BRUSH...(getting louder)

HARRY: Let's look around. What's his costume?

ARVIN: He's dressed as the famous playwright, Shakespeare. He has a black cape and a little goatee.

GILLIAN: I don't see him anywhere.

HARRY: I wonder what happened. Maybe we should go out to the tree and look around.

SFX: CROWD ROARS

ARVIN: What happened to the lights? Who turned out the lights?

GILLIAN: Harry, here's a flashlight.

SFX: CLICK

HARRY: There. Now we can at least see...

SFX: HOP, THUD, BRUSH...

GILLIAN: What's that noise?

HARRY: It's...a...I don't know.

GILLIAN: We need to find Mr. Chad. I'm scared.

ARVIN: Maybe this is part of the play. Maybe Mr. Chad turned out the lights....

HARRY: I don't think so.

GILLIAN: Me either.

SFX: (growing louder) HOP, THUD, BRUSH...

GILLIAN: Harry! What is that? I'm scared!

HARRY: It's coming from the back of the house.

ARVIN: You mean *they* are coming from the back of the house. Look!

SFX: CROWD SCREAMS, CROWD RUNS, DOOR SLAMS.

ARVIN: The crowd is running out the front door, and the toads are coming in the back!

HARRY: They're not like any toads I've ever seen.

GILLIAN: They're huge! Bigger than huge! They're humongous!!

SFX: HOP, THUD, BRUSH

GILLIAN: They're getting closer. DO SOMETHING!!

ARVIN: We're the only ones left! Everyone else escaped!

HARRY: We can't get to the door. They've got us trapped.

ARVIN: There are so many...they're...

SFX: SIZZLE

HARRY: (amazed) Look! Look what happens when I shine the light on them.

GILLIAN: The light stops them! What are those things in the air?

HARRY: Brooms. Floating brooms. There's one behind each toad.

GILLIAN: The brooms are brushing away the toads' tracks!

ARVIN: One broom is glowing!

GILLIAN: We've got to find Mr. Chad.

HARRY: I think we have. That glowing broom is right behind that toad...and that toad is wearing a cape and a goatee!

GILLIAN: Aaahh!!

HARRY: Let's get out of here!

MUSIC: OMINOUS CHASE MUSIC

SFX: RUNNING, SLAMMING OF DOOR

ACT III, Scene 2

EBENEEZER: Harry, Gillian and Arvin run out the front door, but they don't hear it slam. A floating broom holds it open while the toadies pass through.

HARRY: Run to the barn. Hurry!

SFX: HOP, THUD, BRUSH...

GILLIAN: They're after us.

ARVIN: Shine the light on them, Harry!

SFX: SIZZLE

EBENEEZER: Harry, Arvin and Gillian make a mad dash to the barn. The huge, lumbering toadies and their brooms move with amazing speed. One ugly toadie closes in on Gillian. It points its broom at her...

GILLIAN: (screaming) HARRY!

SFX: SIZZLE!

EBENEEZER: Out of nowhere, Harry's flashlight beam crackles on the toadie's slimy green skin. The toadie cowers, and its broom falls to the ground.

In the middle of all of this, Mondo gets out of his brother's car and starts down the farmhouse driveway. He's wearing a leather jacket and sunglasses.

MONDO: (calling out) Hey, Hairball!

HARRY: Oh, no! It's Mondo!

GILLIAN: Come on! Keep running, don't stop!

MONDO: Hey Hairball! I got you now!

HARRY: *You've* got me? Take a number, Mondo!

ARVIN: Harry!

GILLIAN: You guys! Will you come on?

SFX: RUNNING

ARVIN: Hurry! Get to the barn!

HARRY: Whew! Made it. Where's Gillian?

GILLIAN: I'm here. We're all in the barn. Shut the door! Shut the door!

SFX: Heavy wood DOOR SLAMS SHUT

GILLIAN: Harry, quick, slide that metal thing in so it locks.

SFX: METAL LATCH SLIDES

HARRY: There. Is everybody okay?

ARVIN: (obviously shaken) Yeah, of course.

GILLIAN: Yeah.

EBENEEZER: Outside, strange wails from cows, horses and sheep fill the night air. But there are no animals at the deserted farm...

ACT III, Scene 3

GILLIAN: (calling out) Look! There are some old steps going up to the hayloft. I see a window up there.

HARRY: You guard up there. We'll guard down here.

GILLIAN: O.K.

MUSIC: TRANSITION

SFX: WOOD CREAKING

GILLIAN: (to herself) These stairs are kind of rickety. I hope they don't...Aaahh!!

SFX: WOOD BREAKING

HARRY: Gillian!

EBENEEZER: Gillian slips through a hole in a rotten step. Luckily, Arvin is under the stairs and catches her feet. He quickly hoists her up. She pulls herself through the hole and onto a sturdy step above.

GILLIAN: Thanks Arvin...(to herself) Oh, he's gone. (calling out) I'm okay, Harry, I'm in the hayloft.

SFX: FOOTSTEPS CRUNCHING on hay.

GILLIAN: (to herself) What's that in the corner? Is it a toad? No, it's an old cedar chest. I wonder if it's locked...

SFX: HINGES CREAK OPEN

GILLIAN: (to herself) It's not. Look at all these clothes. They're beautiful and so old. This long skirt and this apron and this bonnet, they're...Oh, my gosh! They look just like the costume I'm wearing. They must belong to the Goodwife of Hamstead Farm!

What's this on the bottom? It's a...salt shaker? Yeah, and it's still full of salt. Ouch! A spark!

SFX: ELECTRIC BURST

GILLIAN: An electric shock out of a salt shaker? (calling out) Harry, Arvin, come up here!

HARRY: (calling) Just a minute.

SFX: HOP, THUD, BRUSH

GILLIAN: (to herself) What's this little book? The pages are so fragile and yellow. It looks like a diary. And there's a letter inside.

SFX: UNFOLDING OF PAPER

October 31, 1824

To Thee:

They call me the Goodwife
of Hamstead Farm.
I'm also the Good Witch
who battles harm.

The Evil Witch is captive
in the gnarled oak tree.
One day she will try
to outwit my decree.

She will capture three souls
to break the spell,
and substitute them
in her wooden cell.

To halt her trickery...

SFX: HOP, THUD, BRUSH...

GILLIAN: (scared) Who's out there? Harry? Arvin? Where are you?

SFX: HOP, THUD, BRUSH...

GILLIAN: Harry! Arvin!

EBENEEZER: In the light flickering through the barn window, Gillian sees a toadie.

GILLIAN: Aaahh!! How...How did you get in?

EBENEEZER: The toadie points the bristles of its suspended broom toward Gillian.

SFX: WHOOSH!

EBENEEZER: In a flash of green light, Gillian is vaporized and sucked into the broomstick.

GILLIAN: (gurgling) Aaahh!!

SFX: WHOOSH!

EBENEEZER: The toadie wears a miniature version of Gillian's apron and bonnet. The broom now glows.

Harry and Arvin hear Gillian's scream.

HARRY: Gillian!

ARVIN: Gillian!

SFX: RUNNING UP CREAKY STAIRS

EBENEEZER: Harry and Arvin quickly run up the stairs to the hayloft, narrowly missing the broken step. When he reaches the top, Harry shines his flashlight on the glowing broom. The broom immediately drops onto the hay. The toadie tries to grab it, but is stopped by the light.

SFX: SIZZLE

ARVIN: The toadie can't get the broom as long as you shine your flashlight on it.

HARRY: That's not a broom. That's Gillian!

ACT III, Scene 4

MUSIC: TRANSITIONAL

EBENEEZER: Outside the barn, Mondo takes a pencil flashlight from behind his ear. He shines his light in the toadies' eyes just to irritate them. He obnoxiously jerks the light back and forth, unaware that it's saving him.

MONDO: So what's with the slimy green costumes? You are uuugly! (laughing)

SFX: CROWS CALL. FLAPPING WINGS approach, then fade into the distance. WIND HISSES. BRANCHES BEAT against windows. DOORS RATTLE on their hinges.

MONDO: (scared) What's going on? (calling out) Hey, you guys, open up! Come on, open the door!

SFX: COWS, HORSES and SHEEP WAIL.

MONDO: (really scared) I don't get it. There aren't any animals here...

EBENEEZER: Another toadie hops behind Mondo. A suspended broom sweeps away the toadie's tracks. As the toadie comes closer, the moaning of animals grows louder and more distressed.

SFX: HOP, THUD, BRUSH...

MONDO: Who's out there? What's going on? Hey guys? Let me in the barn. Hey, Hairball...Harry?

SFX: ANIMAL WAILS turn into CROAKING.

EBENEEZER: More and more toadies appear out of the darkness. They back Mondo up against the barn door. He drops his flashlight.

SFX: NOISES STOP

EBENEEZER: A toadie points its broom bristles toward Mondo. In a flash of green light, Mondo is vaporized and sucked into the broomstick.

MONDO: (gurgling) Aaahh!!

SFX: WHOOSH!

EBENEEZER: The toadie wears a miniature version of Mondo's leather jacket and sunglasses. Its broom now glows.

Harry and Arvin cower in the hayloft, watching through the window.

ACT III, Scene 5

MUSIC: TRANSITION

ARVIN: Did you see that?

HARRY: They zapped Mondo into that broom. That's why it glows.

ARVIN: The same thing must have happened to Gillian and Mr. Chad. That's why the toadies wear their clothes.

SFX: A WIND suddenly rises out of the field with a spooky, hollow WHIR.

SFX: In the distance, WHISPERING VOICES chant in an unknown tongue.

SFX: HOP, THUD, BRUSH...

HARRY: The barn door is opening. I thought it was locked.

ARVIN: It was.

HARRY: We've got to get out of here, Arvin.

SFX: THUMP, THUMP, THUMP

ARVIN: They're coming up the steps!

HARRY: Oh, no! Arvin, look out! That big toadie is pointing its broom at you! Duck!

SFX: Green light beam RICOCHETS off the walls.

ARVIN: It just missed me! Harry, pick up Gillian's broom and grab the flashlight! Quick!

EBENEEZER: Harry tries to grab the flashlight, but the big toadie quickly points the broom in his direction. A burst of green light shoots out.

SFX: Light beam RICOCHETS off the walls.

EBENEEZER: Harry dives out of the way. The broom's light zaps a pile of hay behind him, and it sizzles into smoking ashes.

SFX: CHURCH BELL RINGS

HARRY: The big toadie is putting down its broom. They're all leaving.

ARVIN: Look out the window, they're all hopping across the field. They're going toward the gnarled oak tree.

HARRY: We've still got Gillian's broom!

ARVIN: But how do we get her out of the broom?

ACT III, Scene 6

HARRY: We need to know what all this means. We need to know how to get them all back.

ARVIN: Look! Here's an old letter. I think Gillian was reading it.

HARRY: Let me see.

SFX: CRINKLING OF PAPER

HARRY: (reading)

> October 31, 1824
>
> To Thee:
>
> They call me the Goodwife
> of Hamstead Farm.
> I'm also the Good Witch
> who battles harm.
>
> The Evil Witch is captive
> in the gnarled oak tree.
> One day she will try
> to outwit my decree.

She will capture three souls
to break the spell,
and substitute them
in her wooden cell.

To halt her trickery,
you have until midnight.
Conjure me with this spell.
Say it loud, say it right.

ARVIN: Wow! Mr. Chad's play really was true.

HARRY: Here's the spell.

SFX: CRINKLING OF PAPER

ARVIN: It says three souls, and we've still got Gillian.

HARRY: What if we don't get her out of this broom by midnight? What will happen?

ARVIN: She could stay in there forever!

MUSIC: STING!

HARRY: The letter says the gnarled oak tree. We don't have much time. Let's get our bikes.

ARVIN: Ride bikes through the field?

HARRY: It's the fastest way. You take the spell, I'll take Gillian's broom.

SFX: Barn DOOR OPENS, FEET RUNNING

HARRY: My bike has a flat! Somebody poked a hole in it!

ARVIN: Mondo!

HARRY: You ride your bike and take the spell. I'll run with the broom. Go!

ACT III, Scene 7

MUSIC: FAST TRAVELING MUSIC

EBENEEZER: The toadies sit inside the charred circle that surrounds the gnarled oak tree. When Arvin gets near, he stops and hides his bike. He lies down on his stomach, and crawls closer so the toadies can't see him. He holds the spell tightly in his hand.

SFX: CHANTING CHORUS of unintelligible voices.

SFX: EXPLOSION

EBENEEZER: When the smoke clears around the oak tree, there stands the Evil Witch.

EVIL WITCH: Now, as the midnight hour approaches, we must act quickly. Come, my little toadies. Bring forth the jealous brooms.

EBENEEZER: The toadies present their brooms to the Evil Witch. She takes the first glowing broom. The toadie wearing Mr. Chad's black cape and goatee watches proudly.

EVIL WITCH: (chanting) Toona Toona Da Boo.

EBENEEZER: The Evil Witch taps the broom three times. Then, in an instant, Mr. Chad is vaporized into the tree.

SFX: WHOOSH! GLEEFUL CROAKS

EBENEEZER: The Evil Witch takes the second glowing broom and begins her chant. The Mondo toadie, in leather jacket and sunglasses, sits proudly in front of her.

EVIL WITCH: (chanting) Toona Toona, Da Boo.

EBENEEZER: The Evil Witch taps the Mondo broom three times. Then Mondo is vaporized into the tree.

SFX: WHOOSH! GLEEFUL CROAKS.

EVIL WITCH: Three jealous brooms will set me free. Now, for the last one. (pause) Where is the last glowing broom?

SFX: LOW CROAKS

EVIL WITCH: Go find the broom! There's not much time! Go!

EBENEEZER: There's a rustle in the field as Arvin quickly stands up. He holds tightly to the spell.

ARVIN: (reading) Goodwife of Hamstead Farm, come release us from this harm. Teepor Van Tampor.

SFX: THUNDER

MUSIC: TWINKLING, MAGICAL

GOODWIFE: Hello, evil sister.

EVIL WITCH: Who conjured you?

GOODWIFE: Someone who wants you back in the tree.

EVIL WITCH: No! No more...

EBENEEZER: The Evil Witch lifts her hands toward the Goodwife. But as soon as she does, her fingers turn into thin, wispy branches and her skin turns into tree bark.

EVIL WITCH: Aaahh!

EBENEEZER: The Goodwife throws out beams of powerful light that swallow up each of the toadies and finally, the Evil Witch.

SFX: WHOOSH!

EBENEEZER: As quickly as it came, the fiery light disappears. It leaves smoldering patches in the grass where the Evil Witch and the toadies used to be.

When the smoke settles, we see Mr. Chad and Mondo back to their normal selves.

ARVIN: Only fifteen seconds until midnight. Where's Harry with that broom?

SFX: PUFFING, RUNNING FOOTSTEPS

ARVIN: (calling out) Harry! Harry, where are you??!!

HARRY: (in the distance) I'm coming. I'm coming.

ARVIN: Hurry up! You don't have any time!

HARRY: (puffing) I'll make it. Don't worry, I'll make it!

ARVIN: (sadly to himself) He's too far away...He was Gillian's only hope.

MONDO: He's going to have to throw it. Like a javelin.

ARVIN: Yeah, that's right! (hollering) Harry, throw the stick! Throw it, like a javelin!

MONDO: You can do it! Come on Harry!

ARVIN: Throw that stick!

MONDO: Throw it now!

HARRY: I'm going to make it!

SFX: PUFFING, RUNNING

EBENEEZER: Harry looks at his watch, then he looks at the broom. He closes his eyes briefly, then opens them. With all his strength he throws the broom, like a javelin, toward the tree. All eyes are on the broom. It soars through the night sky like a radar honing in on its target.

SFX: A CHURCH BELL rings in the distance. Each CLANG closes in on midnight.

EBENEEZER: Just as the Goodwife is beginning to fade away, the Gillian broom lands at her feet.

SFX: BROOM THUDS

EBENEEZER: She turns and smiles. With all the power she has left, she squeezes a beam of light from her hands and floods it over the broom.

MUSIC: MAGICAL, TWINKLING

EBENEEZER: The light sparkles on the broom, clouding it with smoke. Then a soft breeze clears the air. There stands Gillian.

The Goodwife turns to Gillian and smiles. They are dressed exactly alike.

GOODWIFE: Remember Gillian, you are the *good* sister, not the jealous sister.

GILLIAN: I'll remember.

ARVIN: So, you did just like I taught you, Harry old boy. You closed your eyes, you imagined that javelin soaring through the air...

HARRY: Stick. It wasn't a javelin Arvin, it was a stick—a toadie's broomstick.

MUSIC: STING

THE END

Stay Tuned for Scenes from

CREEPERS Mystery Party Game

Screams at Maybe Mansion!

CREEPERS Mystery Party Game
Screams at Maybe Mansion
Trailer

MUSIC: EERIE ORGAN MUSIC

SFX: FOOTSTEPS, KEYS JINGLE IN THE LOCK, DOOR CREAKS OPEN.

EBENEEZER: Hello, I'm Ebeneezer Stump, and you are? Oh, I see. You are here for a Creepers Mystery Party Game.

MUSIC: STING

This Creepers Mystery Party Game is called *Screams at Maybe Mansion.*

SFX: SCREAM!

EBENEEZER: It's a Movie for the Ear and you are all starring in it! You play one of the suspects, and at the same time, you try to solve the spooky mystery.

Remember, when you hear the sound of three bells...

SFX: THREE QUICK BELLS

EBENEEZER: That's your signal to stop the audio. Then you'll interrogate creepy characters, dig for shocking evidence and search for ghastly clues.

MUSIC: STING, MUSICAL TRANSITION

SFX: CRACKLING OF THUNDER, RAIN AND WIND

EBENEEZER: It's a cold, miserable night on the cliffs surrounding Maybe Mansion. Thunder and lightning pierce through the black sky.

SFX: WAVES BEAT AGAINST THE ROCKS

EBENEEZER: Waves pound furiously against the rocks. It's not a fit night for anyone to be out–human or otherwise...

SFX: WOLVES HOWL

MUSIC: ORGAN MUSIC

EBENEEZER: I'm glad you found Maybe Mansion on this terrible night. I hung a lantern outside the door to help you find your way. In the dark, people's eyes sometimes play tricks on them. They think maybe they see a ghostly mansion perched on the cliff, but then again, maybe not. (He laughs.)

SFX: DOOR CREAKS AGAIN

EBENEEZER: Please, come in. I'll show you to the parlor.

SFX: FOOTSTEPS

EBENEEZER: Not that way! That's the gazebo where... (STING) I'll get to that in a minute. Have a seat, I'll let Mrs. Doppelganger know you're here.

SFX: CLANGING CHIME

EBENEEZER: Mrs. Doppelganger is the owner of Maybe Mansion, which she inherited from her great Uncle Digby. She's very upset about what happened last night in the gazebo. We don't exactly know what happened. Maybe it was a theft, maybe it was—a haunting...

MUSIC: STING

EBENEEZER: Let me tell you the facts. Mrs. Doppelganger was preparing to host an art show here. She has a security camera in the gazebo where some of the valuable art was already displayed. Unfortunately the video wasn't working. But we can still hear everything that went on last night...

EBENEEZER: Now, I'll introduce the suspects.

CROWD VOICES: (GASP!) SUSPECTS! WE'RE NOT SUSPECTS!

EBENEEZER: I'm sorry to have to use that word, ladies and gentlemen. But if you were here at the time of the theft, you must be considered a suspect.

CROWD VOICES: GRUMBLING

EBENEEZER: Let's start with Mrs. Doppelganger, the owner and the innkeeper of Maybe Mansion. Are you ready Mrs. Doppelganger?

SFX: FAST HIGH HEELS APPROACHING

MRS. DOPPELGANGER (crabby New Yorker) Of course I'm ready. I'm always ready. Beds are always made. Meals are always on time. If I say I'm ready, I'm ready. What d'ya want outta me?

EBENEEZER: Well, I...

MRS. DOPPELGANGER: I've got no time, I've got no money. I'd say Uncle Digby, what am I doing this for?

EBENEEZER: And what did he say?

MRS. DOPPELGANGER: He didn't. He just sorta kicked the bucket. I thought it was a magic trick at first...but he ain't that good.

SFX: SLOW, HEAVY BOOTS WALKING

EBENEEZER: Oh! Himmee, you're the handyman at Maybe Mansion, aren't you?

HIMMEE THE HORRIBLE: Yes. People think I'm a horrible handyman. They call me Himmee the Horrible. (Pointedly) Did you know that's what people call me?

EBENEEZER: Well, I'd heard...

HIMMEE THE HORRIBLE: Well, I'm not a horrible handyman! I do O.K. But I am a very good magician.

SFX: THUNDER

HIMMEE THE HORRIBLE: (proudly) I did that, that was mine.

EBENEEZER: Quickly, let's move along to Barbecue Betty, the cook...

SFX: WHOOSH! Then TINKLING OF TEACUPS, SAUCERS.

EBENEEZER: Barbecue Betty? Where did she go? I thought she was just here...

MRS. DOPPELGANGER: Whenever you want her–poof! She disappears. Especially when you need a refill on your coffee–into thin air!

EBENEEZER: But I didn't see her leave the room.

MRS. DOPPELGANGER: She's invisible. You didn't know this about Betty?

EBENEEZER: Next I'll introduce someone I can see. Fernando the Mad Scientist. I understand you are working on a very important secret formula.

SFX: SLOW, HEAVY BOOTS WALKING

FERNANDO, THE MAD SCIENTIST: That really makes me mad. That really burns me up. If I was working on an important secret formula, and I'm not saying that I am, DO YOU THINK I WANT IT BROADCAST TO THE WORLD??!!!

EBENEEZER: I won't say another word.

MUSIC: SEGUE TO VAMPIRUS' T.V. THEME MUSIC

EBENEEZER: Let's meet the popular television star, Vampirus.

SFX: SLOW SLIDING FOOTSTEPS

VAMPIRUS: (Count Dracula Voice) Hellooooo everybody.

EBENEEZER: Hello. Vampirus, why is it that you always wear your vampire costume, even when you're not shooting your television show?

VAMPIRUS: Because I look so extremely good in it. Do you have a problem with that?

EBENEEZER: I just wonder what you're hiding under that disguise...Why did you come to Maybe Mansion?

About Ebeneezer Stump

Ebeneezer Stump appeared at my door one day without an appointment. He had a small black bag that he set on a chair. Out of the bag he pulled a lectern (which was much bigger than the bag, so I still don't know how he managed that).

He set up the lectern on...well, actually–nothing. It floated in the air. And so did he.

Next, Ebeneezer reached down and pulled out a large, heavy book.

The room grew darker and darker... Suddenly, two candles jumped out of the bag and hovered above the book. They sprinkled just enough light on the pages so Ebeneezer could read them.

I sat entranced as Ebeneezer began to speak, first revealing only tidbits and scribbled notes. Then I heard characters' voices, and more than one spooky sound.

Finally, he said, "If you're going to write Creepers Mysteries, Connie, you better get started. First, you've got to get into a creepy mood. Try turning the lights down low and crank the fun up high. Create Creepers Mysteries in the dark, using only your imagination. When you're ready, use this flashlight and write down the lines."

Then he disappeared.

I've kept that flashlight by my side ever since.

Throughout the years, Ebeneezer has continued to appear and disappear at just the right times. He nudges, cajoles and inspires me as I write each Creepers Mystery.

The Creepers characters and I have all become very good friends. And we've all gotten to know the elusive Ebeneezer as well as anybody can...which is not very well at all.

But there's one thing we do know for sure: absolutely nothing creepy can happen without Ebeneezer Stump—and the right lighting.

—Connie Kingrey Anderson
Ebeneezer's Friend

About the Author

Connie Kingrey Anderson has a B.A. in Theatre from the University of Minnesota, and a Masters of Fine Arts in Drama from the University of Georgia. She lives on a colorful cul-de-sac in Minnesota with one funny husband, two furry friends, and three times the average imagination.

Whenever she's in the mood for something fun and entertaining, she jumps into another Creepers Mystery. She hopes you'll do the same...

Visit us online at
www.CreepersMysteries.com

CPSIA information can be obtained at www.ICGtesting.com
Printed in the USA
LVOW11s2151120214

373518LV00001B/30/P